Sun
Need the Sun

Branca Tani

Rosen
Classroom™
New York

Sunflowers grow
from seeds.

Sunflower seeds are
planted in the soil.

Sunflower seeds need
water to grow.

Sunflower seeds need
sunlight to grow.

A sunflower grows in the soil.
It is small at first.

The sunflower grows taller.

It has a green stem.

The sunflower grows petals.
They are yellow.

Seeds grow on the face
of a sunflower.
They are brown.

The seeds fall to the ground.
More sunflowers will grow.

We grow sunflowers
in our garden.
We pick the flowers and
bring them home.

petals

seeds

soil

stem

sunflower

water